Azeman, or the Testament of Quincey Morris

Azeman, or
the Testament
of Quincey Morris

by
Lisa Moore

BLACK
SHUCK
BOOKS

For
Derek Hill and Lynda Rucker,
without whom this slim volume would not exist.

Also for
my beloved Jim Long,
whose heartfelt encouragement
is a constant and wonderful mystery

Editor's Preface

My name is Quincey Harker. I was born to a pair of monster-killers, and named for a third, an American, dead before I drew first breath. He was called Quincey Morris, and this is his confession. I found it scrolled and wedged roughly into the great casket which held my parents' trove of papers: diaries, letters, transcribed conversations, all of which told the extraordinary tale of the much-deserved end of that most fearsome of vampires, called "Son of the Dragon," or Dracula.

The world is by now acquainted with this tale, and I will not belabor it. Suffice to say, I am convinced that my mother never read this troubling addition which you now hold in your hands, and I believe it might have broken her heart had she done so. I can tell you she fairly worshipped the Texan who wrote it, spoke of him in terms of hushed hagiology and would not hear against him a detrimental word.

I do not know how the document came here. It fell perhaps into the keeping of my father, a fastidious librarian at heart, whose disposition would no more allow him to destroy an important document, painful as it might be to those he held dear, than he could take an innocent life, and perhaps he tucked it in with the great mass of typescript for the good of posterity and of truth, in the hope that all those who might be ill-affected by its content would be long deceased ere it came to light.

Indeed, it was only upon my father's death (my mother having predeceased him by some years), while embarked on the task of sorting his affairs, that I happened upon it. Although I have no provenance for it, I wish to state clearly and firmly that I believe the document to be genuine, written by the hand of Morris himself, and its contents to be a difficult relating of a genuine truth.

HERE BEGINS THE TESTAMENT OF
MR. QUINCEY MORRIS, LATE OF TEXAS

The Curse

I took my affliction in youth, perhaps at my mother's breast.

I was conjured into life during the War for Southern Independence, my father home, haggard but stubborn, on conjugal leave. He returned to his regiment not knowing that the seed of my own existence had been planted.

He died, or so was reported, toward the war's end at Spottiswoode, and I was raised in a house of mourning. Fourteen windows lined the north wall of our house, each of them draped in black bunting for what seemed my first several years. An old gris-gris woman I ran across once while travelling the bayous told me I'd drunk despair in my first milk, and there was no fixing that shadow, which haunted like a destined thing – or, as she put it, "a haint that clung hold." I crossed her twisted palm with silver, said "Do what you can for me," and winked, jaunty. She cackled and held the money up to the light as if in blessing, so I thought through her goodwill I might beat that shadow fate.

I can say now with some certainty that I did not.

My father did, after all, come back, and he came back altered.

I suppose all fathers return from war altered; mine was more so. I did not recall him, of course, but I could see it in the way women shuddered when he passed. The way the servants left off speaking mid-word when he shuffled into view, crossing themselves once his back was turned. One time I heard our hostler mutter the word "revenant" after my father's receding figure. When I inquired as to its meaning he said nothing, but regarded me with such pity that I was angry, feigned displeasure at the state of my mount's coat and forced him into a gesture of obeisance. The force of my rage generally has its root planted in the soil of an unnamed fear. In this case, it was a fear which no one dared address, allowing it a breadth and ferocious freedom, and it grew and flourished alongside me, a constant thunderstorm crackling in the background of my youth.

He rarely spoke, this specter they called my father. I remember him as a sort of grey phantom, forever clothed in the tatters of his army coat, his hair hard silver, his skin a dusty pallor. He kept upon his person the moth-eaten hide of an old razorback pig, kept it tied at his waist in summer or slung over-shoulder against cold in winter. His eyes were wide and staring, with some perpetual distraction in them, as if he were forced to view the world through an interference of memory, suspended between him and us like an ongoing parade of ghosts.

My mother insisted that my affliction came direct from him. It always seemed she could perceive it with clearer gaze than I, who only ever saw it in the obliquest sidelong manner, through a glass, as it were, darkly.

During the early years of the war, my father rode with Colonel Bourland's Border Regiment, guarding (some said terrorizing) the northwest, skirmishing with Indians and Unionists. Bourland was a zealot and a hard man, and there was dark talk of atrocities committed, including a thorough government investigation into the incident they call the Great Hanging, when forty-one supposed Union sympathizers hung like so much Spanish moss from the Gainesville trees. It remains the most sizable single lynching in the history of those "United" States, and my father was there, and partook of it, partook from the conquering side, the side of power, the side of berskerking, unthinking blood-carnage.

I believe he enjoyed these nebulous pursuits, tasks which might have troubled the conscience of another man. More, I believe he fed off them, took from their tainted wakes some dark brand of nourishment. My father was a man of some means, not self-made but inherited, and he might easily have bought his way out of service. As it was, he never came home but once in all those sanguinary years across which the war stretched like an unravelling shroud. During that single, short visit, I was conceived.

My mother was a stoical woman, a pragmatist. I only once ever saw her afraid, and in that one moment, she was terrified.

The war was over. My father was home, the South as it had existed was forever lost, and I was still a child, too young to think about any of it. My father was a lumbering presence who kept to his own room. We called it his study, but no scholarship went on there. We none of us knew his activity, but it seemed to involve drinking, and remembering, sometimes raging. He came and went at odd hours, always solitary.

I'd begun sleepwalking. I was seven years old, maybe eight.

There were nights I'd wake myself with the crack of a twig under my bare foot, find myself in my nightclothes at the mouth of the forest, about to lose myself in its mysteries. Mother, annoyed, consulted doctors, then took to locking doors and bolting windows at night for, at that age, I had not the height or strength to undo them, and the only danger was the breaking of the porcelain basin or of stumbling too near to the fire.

It was on such a somnambulist night that I woke myself with trying to open the door to my father's study. After, it was determined that I had wriggled through an unlatched window thought too small to be of consequence, but how I regained admittance to the house undetected, and how I found my way to my father's door, which was reached by way of various portals and back staircases, was anyone's guess. I woke after the knob in my hand was turned, the door fell away from my grasp, and the hulking shape of my father rose up against the light of the fire.

I was so startled I fell backwards, and we gazed at one another in silence.

Blood thumped in my ears. His eyes were alight with some fierce thing.

"Alright," he said. "You may as well come inside, then."

His voice rasped with disuse. He let his head fall, turned, and slumped into his chair as if too listless to sit straight, watching me from under gnarled brows. He tugged the razorback hide around him like a crone's shawl and beckoned to me with one slow circle of his gargantuan hand. His lips stretched back into a smile when I hesitated. The teeth were thick and yellowed, his gums pulled away from them as if he were already embarked on decay, although not yet dead.

"Afraid of me?"

"I'm not afraid of anything," I said.

"You're a liar."

I was lying, and I reddened, got up and stepped into the room, as a sort of penance.

He let his head loll to one side, the hideous smile still stretching his skin. "You have it in you. I can see it."

I misunderstood him. "I don't generally lie."

"You lied because you were scared and ashamed of it, but let that go. I can see a thing in you that will shatter your cowardice and make you master among men."

These words affected me like none I'd ever heard. Every child knows itself to be extraordinary, but soon enough comes to know that no one else sees the truth of it. Was it possible this hollowed-out paternal shell saw me with clear eyes? "I did lie. I was ashamed."

The smile twisted into a feral scowl. "One day you'll know that telling truth doesn't make you righteous. On that day, you'll be a man."

He scowled at the fire awhile, his mouth hung open like he forgot to set it shut. Childishly selfish, I wanted to reset his focus on me. "What is it you see in me?"

"It'll show itself. There's no rush."

Then, still gazing into the fire and moving hardly at all, he told me a story.

I never could recall it afterward, not even the next morning, except there was a snake, and something he called a "malfeasance", and something else, something so forbidden my mind closed against it like a prison door falling shut. I remember feeling hypnotized: the fire, the warmth, the hoarse lull of his words, and I may have fallen back into a slumber because suddenly my mother was there in the doorway, snatching me up off the floor and holding me firm against her, backing me away outside. The last thing I saw was my father's skeletal grin, still sitting, unmoved, in front of the flame, speaking some last words to me. Then she pulled the door shut, silently, and we moved upstairs as quietly as we could, as if trying not to wake some terrible thing.

Once in the safety of the kitchen, she knelt to examine my face. That's when I saw her terror. Her hands shook as they held my cheeks, and there was a despair in her eyes, as if any last wiggle-room for hope was closed up for good.

The final words he'd said to me as she pulled me outside were these: "Every man leaves a legacy, and you are mine."

My father did not reside long among us. He vanished, as suddenly as he had come, into an autumn night in circumstances still under dispute. There had been low-voiced accusations following a series of disappearances: farm animals, returning soldiers, eventually children. That the whispers of wrong-doing were so often directed toward my father's door may have been due to his disagreeable bearing and habits, or there may have been something more in it. In the ongoing welter of chaos following upon Appomattox, death and his henchmen were regular visitors to the entire landscape. The world was realigning itself. Everyday life was a sort of maelstrom, a violence of constant change. Your moral compass is a luxury for calmer times. When a whole existence might dissolve in an instant, "right and wrong" starts to look a pedantic duality, dwarfed by words like hunger, blight, disease.

In any case, the night my father vanished was marred by a fire in Mineral Wells, just up the road, a conflagration which consumed a public house and in which at least three men perished. There were no survivors, and no cause for it was ever finally established.

The Bearskin

There were bear in Texas then. Still are, but the creature is shy and retreats from man, backing always further into mountainous regions where it can find its peace and a good diet of fish and berries.

It was Old Tom taught me to hunt. He called himself a mule-skinner, dressed in leathers in the Paiute style, and always wore a tall beaver hat while in town, which made him stand a good head above the crowd. He told tales for his supper. Men passed the jug around a fire and Tom held forth gladly, entertaining them with stories of mountain men grown so feral by lack of community that they had lost the power of speech, grunting and growling and tearing their meat raw with teeth grown thick and hard like wolves' teeth. When ladies were present, he recounted his own feats of survival: thirty summer days lost in the desert whilst driving mules through waterless chalk flats, he at last stumbled into Carson City and faced the wrath of the mules' owner, all of which he'd either set loose or eaten.

I thought him marvelous.

I took my bear on a sojourn up the Pecos.

It was late. We'd made camp at dusk and were asleep by dark. I woke suddenly, and without apparent cause. The moon was bright, gibbous, hanging above the tree-tops. Embers still smoldered in the fire-pit. Frogs and poorwills sounded their parts in the nocturnal orchestra. While I looked up at the moon, distracted by its brightness, all sound stopped. Every natural thing got quiet.

I sat up fast and scrabbled for my rifle. "Always sleep with your shoes on your feet and your rifle close to hand." Tom was full of gnomic aphorisms, and that was one. Once on my knees with the butt of the Winchester against my shoulder, I sat still and listened hard. There were footsteps. Heavy, lumbering, slow, crackling the dried leaves like so many firecrackers.

A hulking shadow reared up against the night. Its shoulders were rounded and bunched, its back humped over. I could hear it snuffle at the night air, trying to place my scent.

It took but one shot. My hand was steady. It was something I learned early about myself. Regardless of drink or fear, my hand was steady. I caught it square, full in the chest. It grunted one protest, then went down with a clumsy thrashing motion.

The rifle's recoil against my tentative position had knocked me backward onto my sleeping roll, but Tom was up by now, gun in hand. "Did I get him?" I asked.

I watched his silhouette. Rifle at shoulder, he approached the dying mass, still twitching in a heap just beyond the border of our encampment.

I was impatient. "Did I get him?"

He beckoned me to come and look, and I did. I saw fur matted with thick black liquid, a snout pointed high as if still smelling, the face pulled slightly back from the teeth.

"I believe this was a she-bear," Tom said.

It gave me pause. "I don't think so."

"No shame in it. She-bear's as deadly as her mate. Deadlier when there's young 'uns." He put another bullet in her to make sure she was down. The sound of it echoed down the length of the river valley, and made me jump. I peered down the river to where it bent behind the hills, afraid some dark and ancient thing would come roaring up to avenge her death. "Still a few hours until sun-up," he said. "Let's string her up, and we'll gut her then." He pulled up her head to examine her fur. He had to pull hard. The dark mass had already lost all indication it ever lived or breathed or moved around at all. It was nothing but a heap of meat and cloth decorated with a fringe of claws and teeth.

"She'll make a nice rug," he said.

After I crawled back under my blanket, I didn't sleep. I'd been half sleeping when I shot her. The hunched shoulders, the labored breath, the fur standing up along the spine like hog-bristles against the moon. I wondered if, inside my sleepwalking head, it was not my father I shot.

Next morning, Tom showed me how to rope her between two trees, gut her and drain her and take off the skin. She was a fair-sized brown bear, not the huge grizzly I'd have preferred. Still, I carried that skin with me as soon as it dried, carried it every day forward.

To this day I carry it.

My mother and I continued in our usual way, but something had fallen between us, a wall of some kind.

I began to spend as much time from home as I could. It was during this period I was learning the skills which would serve me so particularly in later life: all the tricks of manhood, every active thing. To ride and shoot, to clean my own game with the bowie knife I kept forever at my belt, to build a fire when no proper material was to hand, to glean and relieve the ailments of a mount, to build effective shelter against the elements when they were against me, to throw the riata for both practical purpose and to dazzle onlookers with my dexterity. My restlessness grew as I became comfortable in the world of men. I wanted to be away, to discover what there was to know about the world, about myself in it.

I was hardly sixteen when I took my inheritance and turned my face away from the old house. I believe my mother was relieved to see the back of me.

Striking out on my own was no hardship. I had money, my strength, a hardy constitution, and the charm which comes from a youth spent in a house of women. Furthermore, I mistrusted reliance upon servants, travelling alone whenever I could, else in company with self-sufficient companions.

Jorgao I found on my travels in the Amazon. Raised in the depths of the jungle and familiar with its extremities of hardship, he had embarked young on a seafaring life, and so brought with him on his return to shore a wealth of knowledge and practical skills. Once I had earned his good faith, he attached himself to me as the trustiest of comrades, accompanying me through all manner of danger without scruple or qualm.

I met Arthur Holmwood (later Lord Godalming) in the Mexican territory. Jorgao and I first encountered him in a ravine, literally unhorsed by a panther attack. I took the beast down with two shots – one to lame, the second to finish. We reconnoitred his train of mule-packers, set him astride a fresh mount, and saw him safely into Juarez.

Art was scion to a wealthy house of Germans who'd crossed the water and turned English aristocrats, and he knew a level of privilege which made my own look shabby indeed. Once met, we were difficult to part. He never after undertook an adventure by land in which I was not included in the party. I believe he looked upon our travels as a sowing of oats before he would settle into the destined armchair, hunting kennel, accounting desk and sherry-dispenser of the manor-house. He was a quiet fellow with an easy smile, always ready to be entertained, and I had both a constant hum of energy and the need to expend it, so my adventures and shenanigans became a sort of affectionate game between us.

Blessed with these best of companions, I never felt compunction to sit still for very long, and that was lucky, since I had long since become convinced that something was following me.

I first came aware of it in a pueblo in the mountains beyond Cuernavaca.

I'd been employed by Lord Hartlesby on his third attempt to find the fabled city of gold, a devastating expedition from which we barely scratched our way still living from the jungle. Three of our party were lost. Two packers were caught by mudslide while we picked our way in the rain across a nearly vertical field of boulders, then Fallon, our valued quartermaster, fell prey to a nasty bout of fever. He wandered into the jungle in a delirium, muttering about "stone, blue fire and sacrifice," never to be seen again. The voyage is both horrifying and well-documented, and I will not rehash it here, except to say that it further served to ossify my already cynical view of the common man, rich or poor, with his ridiculous refusal to see the plight of mankind as it truly is: caught inextricably, and each man only for his moment, in a realm in which death is both sovereign and ruthless.

And beyond this, a further truth: that there exists something worse, some worse realm even than death's.

Back among humanity, albeit at its fringes, I separated from Lord Hartlesby at the first opportunity and lost myself in the amiable noise of a tavern whilst I mended. I'd torn open a leg in a tumble down a rapids, and infection is deadly in such a climate. A curandero there tended me, made a paste for my wound and quieted my pain with tobacco and datura.

Between doctor's visits, I drank. I was required to stay off the leg, and sitting still is not easy for me, and consequently I developed a fondness for their alcohol: a strange, sweet-tasting brew, thick like molasses, and put it away as quickly as they could brew it up and pour it in a bowl. You will understand when I say my memories of the place are muddled at best.

I do recall the tavern-keeper gave me a room behind the kitchen, so as to avoid my having to manage the staircase, and that he had a lovely daughter, with hair black as raven down falling past her slim waist. I was the only gringo who had ever lingered long there, and I was observed with curiosity and, I think, a certain amused indulgence. I bought the villagers drinks, regaled them with my stories in my broken, drunken Spanish, let them laugh at me without taking offense.

In moments of solitude, which I had come to abhor, I suffered greatly, not from physical pain so much as from a terrible itch, a psychic demand to be moving. If I sat too still in my quiet room, I was certain I could feel it coming nearer. As if one's destiny approaches at a steady rate, and constant movement is the only sane recourse.

Prostrate in the corner, helpless to stand, drunk on the fumes billowing out from the fire, I watched the curandero at his various tasks and muttered prayers. He scattered leaves on the flames which created a silky smoke with a sickening, opiate smell, a smoke which layered my little room in waves then lifted slowly to roll out at the gap below the ceiling. The fire-pit smoldered with strange green embers, or my sense perceptions may have been unhinged by the smoke, or by the brew he gave me to swallow, not a liquid at all, but an unpleasant, slippery mass, like tobacco stewed in brine.

I spoke aloud in order to break the spell. "Sir," I said, "will you venture a guess at how long I'll be laid up here?"

My voice was a skittish rumbling. He knelt over me and laid a moist cloth across the wound down my thigh. A warmth spread comfortingly across my flesh. His eyes were steady, and seemed, in that strange light, to contain all the colors of the spectrum. "This wound will heal," he said. "I think you know you have another which will not."

His voice was calm. It was a voice that had never known fear. My guts curled with envy.

"I apologize," I said. "My Spanish is not strong."

"You have understood me well enough." He stood up and walked back to the fire, knelt back down to grind leaves in his little stone mortar.

I had understood him. I felt like laughing. "If it can't be helped, then I'm at a loss as to what y'all expect me to do about it." I was speaking not only to him, but to my mother, to the hostler who used to cross himself when I passed him, to every other person who looked at me darkly in my short, dark life.

He ground the leaves without hurry, at a steady rhythm. "It is a spreading malediction. It will infect every person you touch, unless they are very strong, or you are very careful."

I closed my eyes. His words resonated inside the vast, smoke-filled, subterranean cavern that was my skull. "I walk, by and large, alone."

"Even a fatal darkness like yours may be used for good."

I did laugh now, a roiling chuckle that bubbled up from some dark room I'd never looked inside. "I swear, doc, I don't know how you figure that."

I didn't bother to open my eyes again. He'd finished talking, and I guess he'd finished his pounding as well, because he brought another cloth, smelling thickly of summer nights and boysenberries, and laid it across my mouth, singing softly and tunelessly as he did it. I fell asleep thinking of home, of the way the amaranth would scatter all down a hillside as if the seeds had been rolled and grasped hold of the earth as they tumbled. How they seemed to set the scrub desert beneath them on fire.

When at last I was pronounced able to walk – had it been weeks? months? – I packed my things and left without delay, pausing only to pay my bill. The tavern-keeper looked at me strangely and, I thought, with an edge of coldness as he took my note and my last purseful of coin. Then he said a thing I did not understand. "Will your companion be staying on?"

Still plagued by a certain smoky-headedness, I assumed I had misunderstood his Spanish. I was intent upon leaving, however, so shook my head and bade him goodbye.

I was tired of the mountains, the hot, continual wetness of them, the rain, the mud, even the viscous honey of the alcohol. I felt heavied with mildew, my bones swollen and thick with moisture. I wanted to be away, to lose myself in the vastness of a desert, someplace where I could blanch my whole skeleton dry and begin over again.

It was later, several leagues to the north, that a runner caught up to me.

He was what they called a loco, a man not outcast, but "apart" in the village. He worked for white men, when there were any, in menial respects, attached himself to us for our liquor and our money. Because of it, he was mistrusted by his own people, and naturally would never find respect among white men, so he lived without it. It had occurred to me there was a certain freedom in that. He was a liminal character, always smiling, never warm. He had been constant at the tavern during my illness, and I thought I had seen the last of him.

He caught me outside my inn in a border town, waved me down with flailing arms. I lent him my flask and he told me the tavern-keeper's daughter had been found mutilated, or "desmenuzada y desparpajada", as he put it, "minced and scattered". He said it softly, for my ears alone, adding, "You must never return to Cuernavaca."

He smiled, lizard-like, his tongue darting from his mouth obscenely, then turned away to find a tavern. He'd already forgotten me.

Animals feed, one upon the other. There will always be predators, and there will always be prey, and most species fall within both columns, as Mr. Darwin will tell you.

We were travelling the Argentine plains: Jorgao, and Art, with the few gauchos he'd hired to tend his belongings and cook our food, and me. We'd bagged a screamer early in the day, and it was plucked and roasting on a fire at sundown. The pampas are so level in all directions that the days feel longer there, without mountains or trees, nothing to obscure the sun's course, which must make its full, graceful descent right down to flat ground in the west. The unnerving thing about such a landscape is that you yourself are open prey, without protection. If something runs at you, you had better have your rifle at the ready to fell it.

A chill falls with the sun in such a place, and on this particular night there was with its onset a murmur of dissent among the horses. A canny vaquero learns early to trust his mount's sense of self-preservation, and I exchanged a look with Jorgao, who rose up without a word.

We'd camped near a single tree, the only tall plant for miles, an ombu with a decent-sized umbrella of shade, and our beasts were tethered to spikes round its base. He went to lean against its thick trunk, stroking his horse's neck and speaking soft Portuguese to the mules, keeping his senses honed for anything amiss. Art, on the other hand, had partaken of spirits and slept soundly, not entirely oblivious to the possibility of danger, but with the easy complacency of a man who has never known a problem that was not solved for him or swept out of his sight. I knew Jorgao's sleep to be lightly broken, making him the ideal sentinel. Trusting to him, but keeping my weapon close to hand, I also fell into an edgy sleep.

A terrible sound woke us.

It was a screaming in the night, so high-pitched as to approach a squeal. I was on my feet and running before my mind could begin to make sense of it.

By the time I reached the tree, it was over. A stricken mule was prostrate on its side, Jorgao kneeling beside it, holding it fast by its broken tether, murmuring to it. Its great eye rolled up at me in the sort of bewildered terror felt at the end of a life one had believed to be infinite. It'd broken loose, Jorgao told me, broken a leg in its terror, and he'd found it flailing in a crippled panic. With gentle hands, he shifted the face to reveal the side of its neck. There was a bloody welt at the nape.

"Morcego vampiro," he said in a low tone. The words chilled up my spine, although I had never previously heard them. He pointed toward the western sky. "The vampire bat. The blackness which flies. It feeds on life-blood."

As strangely as the words sounded to my ears, it would not be the last time I would hear the like. Years later, in the north end of England, the unlikeliest of places, in a parlor for the genteel and the civilized, my flesh would once more crawl on my bones to hear of another such winged messenger of darkness.

Counting Bristles

I don't know what triggered it. Maybe I was tired of running, sick of knowing that every brave thing I did was a cover for a more fundamental cowardice. I wanted to know the truth of it. I wanted to know what followed me.

Leaving Jorgao to his own adventures, I struck out on my own, seeking out holy men. I spoke to black-robes and ascetics, a Viennese alienist, and antler-wearing tribal doctors who pounded drums and blew strange powders into my face. I consulted a conjure-woman in Louisiana, who kept herbs for both healing and damning tied in bunches to switches crossing her low ceiling. She sent me up a nearby holy mound on a quest to meet with my own self, as I understood it, and have it out. I was to sit inside a circle of stones and take no food or water, only chewing on a root she provided me when I felt thirsty. It tasted like licorice. I sat there for a night and partway into another day, then started to feel like a lunatic and went back down the hill to find something of substance to drink.

I found my answers, at last, in a dilapidated hotel on the Amazon.

I'd returned to the jungle seeking the sacred yage ceremony, but no amount of gold or pleading seemed to open that particular door to me. The natives I approached turned stony-faced, shook their heads, and dissolved back into the jungle. By then, I knew why. They could smell it on me. I was seeking to cleanse a taint which could not be cleansed. I was the Fisher-King, and my wound offended heaven.

Everything was shabby inside the place, but had once been grand, which made its current state more disgusting. Finely-carved wooden pieces were grooved and scratched, their varnish worn off, spiders nesting in their nether corners. Scarlet velvet wallpaper curled away in strips from the wood beneath, now stained with the residue of melted paste. Down pillows, once overstuffed, leaked feathers from invisible rends, and the ornate slip-covers, too fine to wash, showed brown stains through faded patterns of green and red embroidery.

The air was heavy with moisture, and constant sound threw a curtain across the night: birds, insects, every crawling or flying thing seemed to bellow continually.

The first thing I did once alone was to sweep the rich bedding onto the floor and unfurl my own bearskin across the netted rope strung between the bed-poles.

After that, I don't remember much. I drank, then fell into a nightmare in which I clung to a piece of wood in an endless, flat ocean while vultures dove for my eyes.

When I woke in the morning, the room was wrecked. The daintily painted white wicker chairs looked as if they had been torn asunder by teeth. The pillows were heaps of feathers, and even the solid wood was splintered. I was sprawled half on the floor in my bearskin, and a short man with a reddish beard stood over me.

He was burly and his face at rest pulled into a scowl. His eyebrows had a singed quality, as if he sacrificed them working over a hot anvil. His wide elbows bent akimbo, his fists on his wide hips, he surveyed the place with disapproval. He was in mid-sentence when I woke, as if we had been conversing whilst I slept.

"No man is Azeman," he said. He picked up what bedding was left unshredded and began rolling it into careful bundles. "Azeman follows. Clings hold. Finds a man with poison in his veins, and rides him to food."

My throat was on fire, and when I tried to speak, there was no sound. I swallowed with some effort, and tried again. "I'm not from the jungle. How would he find me in Texas?"

He shrugged. "In this place, he is called Azeman. In your country, he will have a different name, but he walks the world over."

He was an unpleasant fellow, with leather for skin and a great mat of yellowed hair, like raw wool left too long crumpled in a dusty attic. He worked at straightening the room, and spoke as if he was describing some mundane species of trout or rosebush.

I climbed to my knees, and decided that was plenty vertical for the moment. "But what is he?"

He found the heavy end-table I had smashed, and made a clicking sound in his mouth, lifting the great hulk of wood with one hand as if it were insubstantial as a cushion. "His food is blood, and female. Mostly, the blood of the female."

"Then what does it want from me? If not my blood?"

A barking laugh erupted from the face. It startled me. He smiled, a lipless stretch of yellow teeth splitting the yellow leather face. "You know what," he said.

His manner startled me, his words frightened me, and I got angry. "You presume to know a good deal."

It was an absurd indignation croaked in a stricken drunkard's voice, but he reacted to it. His teeth vanished, and the thick red line of eyebrow crumpled into a central thicket. In a sudden movement he crossed the floor between us, and before I could lift a heavy arm to defend myself, he pushed his right palm hard against the center of my forehead and I fell backward, as helplessly as a child, as gently as a feather.

I felt an unearthly sensation of being suspended in time and space. Before I hit the floor, I was back outside Cuernavaca, back in the unnamed pueblo, in the humble tavern, sprawled on my sleeping-mat on the floor.

I was reliving a memory I hadn't known I possessed.

The back of my hand knocked over an empty jug, which rolled until a wad of rushes stopped it. I was on my back. My head buzzed with swarming insects, clacked and chattered with flocks of lunatic birds. I was drunk, and sick, and the two states melded into a volcanic miasma of ill intention.

My flesh was clammy with sweat. The room was hot, or maybe the room was cold and only I was hot, because the tavern-keeper's daughter knelt by the fire, stirring its embers into life.

Once I saw her, I could not look away, my head twisted at an angle. She bent forward, jabbing deftly with a long stick. I did not see her face, but I heard her blow and watched the angry orange reaction of the coals to her breath. Her left hand was twisted at the side of her neck, holding the long sweep of her hair away from the flame. Dark, slim hand, black fall of hair, like the sheerest waterfall under the fullest moon. The fingers twisted the hair into a knot, held it fast.

A monstrous emotion rose up inside me. *Vanity* I thought, or some dark thing inside my head did. *Vanity keeps her hair long, against all practicable consideration.*

I rolled off my mat onto one elbow, and reached up a hand.

It took her by surprise, and she nearly jolted forward into the fire to escape it. She was nimble, though, and slid sideways into the room while I pawed clumsily at the floor, trying to right myself. I laughed at my own clownishness and got to my knees, facing her.

Her head was lowered, eyes black with emotion, her voice chanting low and constantly in her own language, not Spanish, but the Indian dialect indigenous to the place. She might have been threatening, or pleading, or praying to her gods. The words sounded ancient, part of the land itself. They lulled at me like the lapping of waves against sand. I liked her voice. I liked the fear in it.

I was up now, on my knees and ready. I stretched my arms out wide to either side. The room was narrow and she would have to brush past me to reach the door. I leered. It was a game.

She feinted toward the fire then tripped ably across my sleeping-mat on the other side, and I dove the wrong way like a goalkeeper fooled on his line. Once in the doorway, she spun back around, her eyes all fury, and spat. "Azeman," she hissed at me.

It was an accusation. I didn't know the word, but now I was also furious, and threw myself forward onto my front, hissing my own foul names at her and reaching one long arm forward to catch at her ankle.

There was a broomstick propped next to the door. She pulled her foot out of my reach, knocked the broom across the doorway, and was gone.

I scrambled after her, but once through the doorway, I stopped.

The malevolence was gone. As suddenly as it had come on, the violence I had felt toward the girl flooded away. It was as if by crossing the threshold, I had become another person.

She ran, and I let her. Befuddled, I turned and looked back into my little room, now red-gold with firelight. The upturned broom still lay across the foot of the doorway, and something else was there with it.

Its shape was vaguely man-like. It was grey and black, like a great lump of coal, but although its edges were defined, the colors shifted, as if made out of smoke enclosed within a transparent skin. The creature made a snuffling sound edged with throaty growling, a thing I've heard from bears and pigs whose breaths come raggedly through snouts. It crouched on bent knees and elbows, its featureless face pressed close to the broom, its spindly wisps of fingers threading themselves methodically through its bristles, as if intent on arranging them.

I widened my eyes then squinted in attempt to focus, certain I must be seeing wrong. I stood a mere few yards from the thing and suddenly felt enormously tall, or that gravity was pulling at me more insistently, inviting me toward the floorboards myself. I fought the urge and stayed upright.

Suddenly, the thing lifted its featureless face toward me and froze. The snuffling stopped. It had no eyes, but I knew it watched me. A horrible stench filled the room, like meat left to rot in a hot tin box, and I turned, panic-stricken, to run, scareder than I've ever been in my life.

I woke out of the memory with the kind of sound a man makes when he's trying not to drown. I was back with the dwarf in my broken-up room. He was looking at me calmly, his arms crossed at his chest.

"What was it?" My voice was hollow and ragged as I felt. "Was that…?" I stopped. I couldn't ask it. Instead, I pushed myself back up into a sitting position and said, "What was it doing?"

He said, "Are you sure you want to know?"

I wasn't. "Tell me."

He shrugged and went back to straightening the room. "It was counting the bristles."

I was going mad, or he was. "It was doing what?"

"She knocked the broom across the doorway for a reason, knowing that the Azeman," he turned and pointed a finger at my chest, "at that moment, would feel compelled to count each of its bristles before it would cross the threshold."

I felt the emotion flood out of me in a wave, leaving me curve-backed and relaxed. I laughed. "I am mad."

"It fools the Azeman," he said. "It's an easy trick. It can be done with a scattering of seashells, or a spilled bucket of sand. It buys your intended victim time to escape."

My intended victim. The laughter went out of me and I was sober as an altar-boy. "How do I stop it?"

He turned his weirdly golden eyes on me and tilted his head to one side, looking like a bird. One of those mean-looking, hunch-shouldered water-birds who could take you down with one thrust of its beak. He was deciding something about me.

In the end, he pointed at my bearskin. "Azeman manifests within the skin of the totem." I clutched the bearskin without meaning to. I owned few possessions, but the ones I valued were my rhino-horn bowie knife and the skin I took that night in the hills off the Pecos River. "You salt the skin," he went on, "and Azeman cannot use it."

He watched me, and I became aware that I was clutching the fur so hard that my knuckles were white. A slow smile spread evilly across his face. "But you will not salt it. You will not burn it. You will not even stow it someplace away from you." He made a derisive, snorting sound. "Before nightfall, you will forget everything I say."

I did not speak. I hated him, but he didn't care about that. He went back to pecking through the room, trying to salvage what was salvageable.

I overpaid for the damages, and left the place as soon as I could ride.

England and Dracula

It was, of course, in England where my destiny awaited me in the person of Miss Lucy Westenra. Or, rather, Art met her first, fell in love with her, then introduced her to both me and Jack Seward, the doctor who'd been our medical companion on an excursion into Ceylon. Afterward, I'd tagged along with them back to Whitby where Jack lived, more for want of any more pressing destination than for love of England, which I found tiny and aggressively civilized, without wide open spaces, without jungle or tangle. Everything manicured, muscled into shape, cut to exact size and proportion.

Lucy, though, was different. Red-haired, red-lipped, pale-browed, thin as a gently-curved bannister-rail, she was draped by a bevy of chambermaids in an endless parade of gowns made from ridiculously fine silks. She sprang from that finely-honed, upper-class echelon of behavioral niceties, yes, but there was something hot and alive in that lithe, pale body, something unpredictable and entirely intoxicating. She was a snap-dragon among the daisies, an orchid amid the milkweed. I told her so. It's true, I said things like that, privately and close to her ear. She enjoyed my impertinences. They made her laugh, and I became utterly addicted to her laugh, the sound of it and what it did to her face, the curves and lines and muscles it brought to life there.

I won't pretend any special insight or sensitivity in my newfound obsession: every man who ever laid eyes upon her wanted her. I also would take no offense if you were to imply that my heart might not have been so readily bestowed had my friends not already been fully invested in the same direction. Art had her in his sights right off, and any fool could see that Jack Seward was besotted. Still, give my heart I did, and once you've taken the wound, it'll fester without its due attention, so I mooned and went feverish and carried on with the rest of them. Art said she was "of high birth and finest breeding," by which I guess he meant she had the makings of a prime brood-mare, and was to be kept in a sturdy-walled stable pending her time in pasture, a stable whose door could withstand the brutal hooves of impatient stallions such as we.

In short: I proposed, and she turned me down, accepting Art instead.

It made sense. They were peas in a pod, critters from the same pond. They both knew what fork to use, and the polite way to address a viscount as opposed to a bishop. I wished them both well, sincerely so, and set out on walkabout, round about the lake country and into Wales, where the town names are so complicated with so few vowels that it's in its way like navigating a jungle.

I took some drink during this time, enough to quell a rising tide of something akin to panic. In thrall to Miss Lucy, I'd sat still longer than was my custom, and I was starting to kick at my stall some. In a place called Tergerthen, approaching the southernmost part of that claustrophobic island, I was making arrangements to ship out as far as Massachusetts aboard a newly refitted steamer when Art's telegram found me.

Something was wrong with my Lucy. He was called to his father's deathbed, and Lucy was alone in Jack Seward's care.

For once in my life, I didn't jump up and ride. I sat down, drank another whiskey, and considered. I'd known, even as I courted her, that asking her to share my life was a selfishness. That I was asking an innocent girl to walk into a world of shadows and poisons whose dregs she would never fully shake off, even if she shook away from me. The telegram, with its vague insinuation about impending trouble ("HAVE NOT HEARD FROM SEWARD FOR THREE DAYS STOP TERRIBLY ANXIOUS STOP CANNOT LEAVE STOP FATHER IN SAME CONDITION STOP SEND ME WORD ABOUT LUCY"), brought back the old fears. Servants shuddering as I passed. A half-wit drunk warning me away from Cuernavaca. A tavern-keeper's daughter dead. A broom kicked across a doorway, and a writhing shade with a chilling compulsion to count its bristles.

I wondered if my presence would not make things worse. More darkly, I wondered if I had not been somehow its unwitting cause.

In the end, I went back. Of course I did. A beautiful girl, a girl I loved, was alone, vulnerable, in a house without men, only doctors.

When I arrived, Jack and his Professor Van Helsing welcomed me by rolling up my sleeves and siphoning off my blood to pump into Lucy's pale, prone body. "A brave man's blood," the Dutchman crowed, "is the best thing on this earth when a woman is in trouble."

I did hesitate, I promise you. I even came near to telling them about the possible horrors swimming in this particular brave man's blood, but in the end the idea of seeing it into Lucy's veins was too sweet to resist. Maybe, if she was strong enough, we might create a darkness of our own, after all.

Not long after that, she was dead.

And then, she was up and walking around again.

And so, we arrive at the Count himself, the very fellow to whose fate all our own fates are presently tied.

Only twice was I to lay eyes on him at close range. Three times, I expect, if you ask me again a few days hence, by which time I expect the chips to have fallen in their wanton way, and one side or the other, monster or mortal, will be left standing.

The First Encounter

We faced him first, innocuously enough, at his Piccadilly house, in the very gullet of London.

The funny thing is, because we'd been nervous as cats about getting into the place without drawing attention, we hadn't a notion of a plan as to how to proceed once in. In the end, Art pulled his lord-of-the-manor routine and gulled a locksmith into opening the place for us.

It was very much like a tomb, a man's fist deep in dust, dourly festooned with cobwebs. The only sign of habitation was a heavy oaken table in its central hall crowded with bundles of paper, titles and deeds alongside a fair stack of money, bills and coins intermingled in careless heaps. The rest was must, and the rapid scratching sound rats make inside walls, as if always in a hurry.

And, of course, the coffins.

They were there, too, in the dining room, eight of them. We threw open the windows to let in the wan light, for it was a typically cloudy London day, then we set about destroying the erstwhile beds through sanctification. This could be accomplished in a few ways. The Dutchman liked to wrest them open and douse and sprinkle them with his holy water and his broken wafers, drape them with his cruciform contraptions and garlic flowers. In a rush, the same end could be accomplished by firing a "sacred" bullet through the lid, making the dirt inside somehow inhospitable to the vampire's rest; I never knew how. I suspect the touch of it burned him as volcanic spew would burn a man.

Since I was the marksman of the bunch, I'd been formally presented with a few of these "sacred" bullets, but the echo of a gunshot was too risky in such crowded territory. London is not like Texas. You can search the length and breadth of the place and never once see a man sporting a sidearm.

A knock came at the door.

The moment was almost comic, how we all froze in our lid-prying and water-sprinkling and looked blankly, a little guiltily, each at the other, like schoolboys caught in a secret smoke. It was an economical rap, though, the knock of the delivery-boy, not an enemy. I gestured everyone back out of sight, and with a swing of my chin guided the professor to the door.

He returned with a telegram. Mrs. Harker sent word that Dracula himself, taking advantage of the overcast afternoon, was on his way to the very house. Van Helsing was still calculating how much time we had to prepare when we heard the carriage pull up to the curb. After a minute, we heard the driver's "hup" to his horses, and the even rhythm of the hooves started up again and faded into the street noise.

Then a key turned in the front lock.

Wordlessly, I pointed each man to his position around the room, each to a doorway or a window. My thought was to trap the creature between us, but beyond that, I had no plan. We armed ourselves, some with crucifixes and saint-bottles, some of us with more conventional weapons. Harker had drawn his Gurkha knife, somewhere between a scimitar and an Australian boomerang, and I felt the security of my Colt in hand, the Dutchman's God-blessed, devil-damning bullet in its chamber.

We waited an eternity for the door to open. There were no footsteps. Not a sound.

Art and I exchanged a grim look. Our prey had scented us. I tightened my grip on the Colt, felt for my knife-butt with my other hand.

Without warning, the door flung open and Dracula leaped in, an unholy leap, more than halfway across the room, snarling as he landed. My arm was up instantly, but the way we were arranged, I could not fire without endangering my companions. While I pulled my knife instead, Harker lunged with his, and the Count made an agile sideways step, losing only a vest-button and a scrap of fabric to the blade. He regarded us coolly, reconnoitering, counting us. Assessing the enemy force.

I saw his next move in his eyes as clearly as if he spoke it, and ducked out the back door just as he dove for the nearest window. I heard the glass shatter behind me as I pounded down the stairs toward the garden.

Art was on my heels. Without a word, I pointed him down the mews while I bolted for thc stable. Half its front gate swung easily open and closed, thump, open and closed, thump, as if in a crossways breeze. I caught it open and looked in through the gap at the hinge. The doors at the far end were closed. I stepped inside and latched the door behind me, then stood silent and immobile, my revolver drawn, while my eyes adjusted to the darkness.

The day was gone. Twilight came fast. We were travelling in the beast's realm now.

The place was clearly empty of horses, no doubt had been for some time. It lacked that zestful pungency which equine life brings to enclosed air. As I stood, I heard nothing, saw nothing beyond the slowly-emerging ghosts of stalls and beams, ancient hay tracked across a packed-dirt ground. Still, I kept quiet. Back at the house, Harker and Seward exchanged raggedly urgent whispers. A flustered pigeon rustled and worried in the height of an eave.

There was no movement, no sound, and yet I felt he was there. I moved carefully to stand sideways, cocked my piece and aimed it straight down the center path at the opposite door.

I said, "You're a quiet fellow, I'll give you that."

All at once, the far doors fell open wide with a pair of wooden thumps. I don't know what kept me from firing at the sudden noise; nine out of ten men would have done it in the circumstance. Somehow, I held back.

A tall, top-hatted silhouette reared up against the city-night beyond, the gas-lit, carriage-ridden streets of London, all oblivious to this malefaction infesting its heart. He was long and long-limbed, his slender arms held outstretched, still touching the doors on either side. Long, straight hair slicked down the sides of the slender neck which ended in an upright collar. Beyond these and a stylishly flaring coat, I could see no details for want of light.

He lifted his face with a small jerking motion, then held it still again, uptilted very slightly, as if trying to place a scent.

We stood like that, predator and prey, both of us testing the air, venturing to glean which of us was which. Then a horse-drawn hansom swung around the curve before the house and its lantern sent a flash of light across the wall. I saw his eyes then, reflecting ice-cold white, as wolves' eyes do.

The dark was no obstacle to him. He was watching me.

Then he spoke. "You know your cowboy toys will not kill me."

His voice was quiet and smooth and sounded, disconcertingly, as if it came from right beside my ear.

I adjusted my aim downwards. "Might slow you down apiece, though," I said. "It's hard to run without knees."

He laughed, one sharp hiss. "You are different."

"Yes, I am," I said, and pulled the trigger.

It misfired. I swear to God, that Colt has served me well and truly for twenty-odd years. I clean it and care for it like it's my own flesh and blood, and that is the only time it ever let me down.

I cursed and ran at him, roaring out a rebel yell, just as I'd learned it from old soldiers at home. My blood was up.

He didn't move, not a flinch.

I ran bent forward and knife drawn, ready to come up below his chin and drive it home clear through the neck.

With a small motion, he lifted a bag of coins from his pocket and scattered them across the stable's threshold, then took one long step backwards.

It was like I came up against an impenetrable wall of cloud and smoke. All I could see were the coins on the ground, shining at me in an unearthly way. Every other thing went clean out of my head: Dracula, my companions, my vengeance for my killed sweetheart, all gone.

When Art found me, or when he woke me, I should say, because it was just like he coaxed me back from some far-distant place, our enemy was long gone, and I was on my hands and knees in the dirt, snuffling like a pig, counting those goddamned coins.

We rejoined the others and set out to protect Mrs. Harker, as it was night now, and she vulnerable. To his credit, Art never said anything about it, not to the others, or to me. To this day, I don't know how much he suspects about my malediction. He is too much the gentleman to address the subject.

The Second Encounter

Blood was everywhere.

Harker lay sprawled in a stupor. A night-creature controls sleep, and Harker was in this one's power. While Dracula was present, Harker would not wake, and the creature was most assuredly present.

He stood at the bedside, a long, billowing swath of black silk. Only his face and hands emerged from darkness, and they were horribly white, the white of a whiskered bottom-feeder whose life is spent at such a depth the sun never reaches it. The white of maggots, of dead things, and leprous.

One taloned hand held both Mrs. Harker's arms back-stretched to keep her immobile, while the other pressed her face against his own breast. His hand was unnaturally long, all tendon and white skin, no meat to mediate its angles into curves. Its fingers tapered into thick claws, and I saw by the ridge of muscles roping along its back that he was pressing her face to himself with enormous strength. There was no chance that she might resist. Indeed, my first thought was that she might suffocate at the front of his suit.

When he came aware of us, he released her, and I saw with some excitement that my fears had been misplaced. His shirt-front was opened at the chest. Her pale face was a smear of blood. He had been feeding her, as a bitch feeds her whelp.

The professor had his host and crucifix to hand. The Count snarled but backed away, letting the bloodied woman fall to the bed on which she had been kneeling. He retreated into the shadow with a beetle-like, scuttling motion. Jack and Art, following the professor's lead, brandished their own cruciform weapons, but a crucifix emptied of faith is like a lantern wanting oil. I almost felt sorry for them. From his shadowed corner, I saw the creature's blood-engorged, wolfen eyes turn to me.

I lit a match and struck the light at the mantel. As his corner was illuminated, the count appeared to crumble into a fine, gleaming powder, a gold-dust scattering on a breath of wind, taking for an instant the shape of a swirling dust-devil, which then blew out at the French door. The last thing to remain of him was the red glint in his eyes, which remained fixed upon my own, and then this also was gone. Nothing left but the bad seed from which grows a nightmare.

The professor and the doctor turned their attentions to the desperate couple upon the bed, while Art stood silently by. I could see his thoughts were grave, thoughts of my Lucy.

I did feel sorry for them.

I slipped outside, quiet but unhurried. The moon moved out from behind a cloud. She was a thick crescent, evoking visions of Turks, of crusades and scimitars, and death by holy zeal. She looked down on mankind with her customary indifference.

I stepped into the shade of a tangled yew-tree from which I would not be seen from the house. I wrangled the pouch from my vest-pocket, bit off a chunk of tobacco, and waited.

A gurgling scream filled the night, like a man choking on molasses, then was broken off into sudden silence. It came from Seward's madhouse, from the fly-eater's window. I pushed my tobacco-pouch back into its pocket and waited some more.

I felt his presence before I saw him.

His black clothes seemed evanescent, all shine and no substance. He didn't step out of the shadow so much as he unfolded from it. He was consubstantial with it, made from its same quintessence. He was tall, erect, weirdly still.

I said, "You killed the woman I loved."

A sound came from his throat, part purring, part clicking. I couldn't tell if it was laughter or something more animal. "I offered her eternal life," he said. "Your sanctimonious friends killed her."

I pulled my knife from its sheath beneath my coat. I did it smoothly, slowly. I'd been a hunter long enough to know that with some beasts, a man won't last a minute in a quick fight. I said, "I've gutted bigger critters than you with this."

He wasn't scared. I didn't expect he would be. He pulled his lips away from his teeth – thick and sharp, like a hyena's, but positioned in jagged layers, like a shark's. He opened his mouth wide to give me a good, long gander. I don't know what I'd expected, but it wasn't that. I don't mind telling you the hair stood up on my neck and my skin crawled with a life of its own. He closed his mouth slowly once he figured I'd got the point and said, "Somewhere may be an instrument of my destruction, but it will never be a man who knows only half his own nature."

I changed the subject. "You snuff the fly-eater?"

He sneered, and I thought of a statue I once saw in French Indochina, a cannibal god carved into ivory. Dracula's was a face carved out of pale disdain. "Men are weak," he said, "and women are food."

Perhaps imprudently, I asked, "And what am I?"

I should not have asked it, but I wanted to know what he knew. I wanted to hear him speak the word *AZEMAN*. Instead, he said nothing. The contempt in his face was a victory. It glowed in his eyes. In that moment, we both knew he'd beaten me.

Without bothering to respond, he vanished. He folded back up into his shadow until he was part of it, and the shadow was all there was.

I went back into the house.

They were still there, the five of them, fluttering with the high emotion charging the nightmare's wake, this nightmare which had for a moment dragged itself into life using us as its chess-pieces. I watched them: Van Helsing, reverting to his native tongue, his high-pitched voice squeezed even higher with emotion, every third word of his already pidjin-English now Dutch and incomprehensible to us; Jack Seward, medical bag a-gape, wielding his sleep-inducing hypodermics as if science were trying to mimic Dracula's own supernatural power; Harker, stunned and impotent on the bed, his blood-smeared wife fighting down her own well-earned hysteria to care for him. And Art, the mighty lord of the manor, standing always slightly apart, assuming the stance of action without ever actually leading. Supposedly, he bore the mantle of paternal power, that avuncular love of the Empire for its subjects, but in the end, nothing would ever really touch him. He did love my Lucy.

I believe that. I know he believes it. But I also saw the look in his eyes when he hammered a sharply-whittled chair-leg through her heart.

Something clicked for me, standing in that bedroom. You could say I suffered an epiphany. You're only afraid when you have something to lose, and I was no longer afraid.

I told them I'd seen a bat flying west, away from Carfax Abbey. They believed me because they were afraid not to. They were pathetic, frail, human. Yes, I pitied them, but there was something underneath it. It's possible that pity always keeps a hidden underbelly of contempt. Anyway, that has been my own experience.

The vampire requires an invitation before it will enter into its pursuit. The professor told us as much, and therein, it seems to me, resides the brilliance of its method.

In the end, Dracula may be nothing more than a ravening beast sated with carnage, but it always begins with some small collusion. It has not escaped my attention, for example, that Mrs. Harker only came plagued by the Count's visits after we left her alone. We excluded her, we five men, her companions who had hitherto kept her privy to every detail of our war councils: one day we proclaimed her temperament too delicate to bear up under such a responsibility and shut her out entirely, for her own good, of course.

That is when the beast moved in, preying upon her in her time of weakness. This irony has not escaped me.

Mrs. Harker was a thin girl, her figure weedy and without substance. Hers was the wan complexion of the English girl raised with too little sunshine, exercise, or affection. Her hair and eyes were dark, more in a bovine than an exotic way. She smiled too brightly and almost constantly, begging scraps of approval from friend and stranger alike.

I use the past tense because all this has begun to change. Since that night of the blood congress, she (like Faust, and like myself) hath two souls dwelling within her breast. The nice girl is still there, ridiculously anxious to be useful, but she lives now entwined with a dark sister, a nocturnal twin which lurks, biding its time. Sometimes you can see it looking out at you from behind those soft, brown eyes. You recognize it by its air of contemptuous amusement, quite alien to the old, stodgy Wilhelmina, who would be rightly shocked by it.

I have found myself, since that night, drawn to her. Some dark thing from another century has taken root within her flesh. We two (should I say four?) are simpatico now in a way we had not been previous. There have even been physical changes: a certain robustness, a new rosy hue which floods at certain times into her cheeks and lips.

And, of course, the scar.

It is a great welt imprinted upon her brow, as if she'd fallen asleep with her face pressed against the edge of a flat iron, except that it never fades. Sometimes, as in the mornings when the professor mesmerizes her to access the recesses of her dark master's mind, the scar will inflame, engorge with her lifeblood. I watch it throb as, eyes closed, she speaks of hearing water lap at wood and masts creak against wind. These trances have dwindled in effect the closer we draw to the devil's actual playground. She has begun bounding out of them with an aggressive cheerfulness, apparently desperate to make us all a cup of tea. Beneath the façade, though, lies a mocking threat, and the scar is always red now, like some worm-like creature attached subcutaneously below her hairline.

It is the mark of Cain. She knows it. We all do.

Once our train alit at Galatz, I took the opportunity to escort her to our hotel whilst the other gents approached the local bigwigs concerning permits and whatnot. The Count's entourage had passed through some days prior. We'd been caught on the back foot, but in my experience, the best hunt is never the one that comes easily.

I carried her bag and steered her through the station, my free hand very lightly touching her elbow. Galatz is an ancient port-town on the Danube, and the towers and spires of many powerful old churches puncture its skyline. I wondered if this flamboyant show of sanctity weighed heavily upon her, but she chattered in her usual manner about nothing at all, and her true thoughts were indiscernible. I found her clattering need for the constant affirmation of smiles and nods and encouraging questions to be exhausting, and I very soon wanted to be free of her. Yet I persisted, and when she fixed upon a compact typewriting-machine in the crowded window of a market near the university, I gallantly took her in and purchased the thing for her.

She looked at me then as if I were Lancelot, or some golden god, and I am not, I assure you, immune to flattery. Bearing both her burdens now, I opened the door and bowed her out ahead of me with a slightly ironic smile, which was good for the usual approving giggle.

The shop was built into the face of one of those great stone walls one finds in cities with long histories of occupation and revolt. A beggar sat against it just outside the door, his blind eyes turned white against the sky, one scrawny talon continually lifted palm-up in a slight circling motion as he murmured the perpetual beggars' chant.

As is my custom, I shook a coin from my waistcoat pocket and dropped it into the cupped palm. I think you and I are enough acquainted by now that you will know the habit springs not from kindness but from some vague superstition that my scattered coins might buy some providential good will.

He let the coin slide with a clatter onto the paving-stones, and I felt his finger-bones clasp hard around my wrist.

He stopped chanting.

Instinctively, I tried to pull away. His grip was strong.

He spoke some words in a loud, clear voice. I know no eastern languages, but Mrs. Harker's face furrowed in concentration. She spoke a few guttural words back to him, then said to me, "This man says he has a message for you."

My body went cold from crown to foot. I could not muster a laugh, but a cynical smile is always easy enough. "Ye gods, man. Have we acquaintance in common?"

She did not smile. She was listening to the beggar, who spoke now rapidly some ten barbarous-sounding words which he repeated twice more, and exactly. When he finished, he released my arm and fell silent, crossing his arms on his knees before him.

Mrs. Harker regarded me with an unwavering gaze which sent through me a quick shock of shame.

"The message is this," she said. "IT SAYS THAT WITHOUT ITS HELP YOU WILL NOT LAST FROM ONE MIDNIGHT TO THE NEXT." Her face creased in thought. "The grammar doesn't hold, does it? The message is from 'it', not 'him', and yet I'm sure I got it right."

She gave me one of her too-bright smiles. This time it made me uneasy.

"You are awfully deft with the language," I said.

Neither her smile nor her eyes wavered. "You forget, I was here before. I rescued my husband from the clutches of a terrible darkness, don't you remember?"

I could see it now. It was smiling at me, the arrogant she-thing which hunkered inside her. It knew my secret, and mocked it. My blood ran ice beneath her gorgon gaze. I said, "Ask him if it is here with us now."

She turned her face toward the beggar and threw some words at him. He did not respond. He sat, indifferent, turned to stone. She looked back to me, her smile a mere hint now. Supercilious as it was, it was perhaps most honest smile I'd ever seen from her. Even as it chilled my blood with its threat, it called me to life.

Without looking away from her, I took a second coin from my pocket and flipped it at the beggar. "Say a prayer for me, compadre."

He let it fall. The clatter of it echoed in the street and he let both coins lie. As we moved away, I looked back at him. Grubby children had already moved in to fight for the money. The blind man himself moved no muscle, made no sound. He looked like a wingless gargoyle which had for one moment come alive to bear messages from empyrean gods.

In light of this extraordinary exchange, Mrs. Harker seemed altered. She carried the typewriting-machine herself, swinging it easily as we walked, and tucked her free hand around my arm with a throaty giggle so that we walked at intimate proximity, her characteristic physical timidity entirely forgotten. I knew the dark twin was in ascendance. This was my moment.

"How much do you know?" I asked, as casually as I could muster.

"Why, Mr. Morris, I don't know what you mean."

I stopped cold and looked at her. I would have sworn the voice was my Lucy's.

Mrs. Harker smiled up at me, raising her eyebrows in a gesture of innocence.

We were around a less-populated side of the hotel. Silently, I pushed her backwards and held her against the wall. "How much do you know?"

She laughed. Her smile was hard, all diamonds and rubies and no warmth at all. The scar on her forehead throbbed scarlet. She leaned her head back and let her lips part in invitation, just as Lucy once had done.

I didn't kiss her. I let her go and backed away. "I talked to him once, your carrion-maker. He called women food."

A horrible leer spread across her face. For a moment, she didn't look woman, or even human. She came close and locked eyes with me, then rearranged her mouth into a prim pout. "I just want to be useful," she said.

Then she pushed past me with the flirtatious sweep of a flower-girl in an alley, and skipped up the hotel stairs.

I left her bag outside the door to her room, loathe to knock. Settled into my own chamber, I worried that she might disclose my secret, or taunt me with it. She did neither. In fact, when we all met at supper, the succubus was gone and Mrs. Harker was again herself: face a little haggard with worry, pinched at the corners of the eyes, always watching us in her predatory fashion, looking to pounce on any half-empty teacup to replenish, or laughing too adoringly at the smallest joke.

Our stay at Galatz was our last within the bounds of the civilized world as we know it. From thence, our party split as we dogged the Count's retreat up an arm of the Danube in a three-pronged attack: Art and Harker by steam launch, Jack Seward and I more swiftly on horseback through the treacherous paths shadowing the right-hand bank, the professor and Mrs. Harker by carriage up the Borgo Pass.

Jack and I brought extra horses along to provide for an overland return for the whole party, in the event of a triumph. (In case we lose, I've told the horses openly, they're on their own to wend their way home. They don't seem concerned at the prospect.) As a precautionary measure to allay suspicions, we took on two locals to ride with us as far as the western mouth of the Borgo Pass, where we plan to leave them, well-enough recompensed to purchase return conveyance with plenty to spare, and we'll continue alone toward the castle.

Our horsemen are Grigore and Tomas, a father and son, both obviously well used to the saddle. These men are Slavs, of the same brand of workman that Dracula must have hired to sail him upriver until his box of dirt might be handed over to his faithful gypsies. They wear short-legged, baggy trousers and coarse linen shirts beneath draping vests, and Grigore, the elder, wears black moustaches so long they overhang his jawline. They are grateful for the pay, I know, but seem to carry suspicions as to the work itself. This may be our doing, as Van Helsing played his cards close to the chest when he hired them. Then, of course, neither Jack nor I speak their language, although Jack can stumble along with them in his medical-school Latin, which I suppose they know from the church. I catch hold of the occasional word, made familiar from my grasp of Spanish and Portuguese, but mostly I read their eyes. Anyway, they would be our companions for a few days only.

Last night, Tomas made the fire, practically a bonfire. "To keep the wolves humble," he said, through Jack's translation. Once we were settled in with warmth and grub, his father brought out a small wind-instrument and began to pipe a soft air.

I was lulled into a peaceful state, but kept lurching into consciousness. I kept catching motion in the trees, heavily shadowed now from the fire's glare. I thought I saw human figures, small of stature, lurking, bending out to watch us. More than once I heard whispering. After I'd walked out to explore then resettled by the fire after finding no trace of intruder, Tomas, the younger, noticed my nervy state and said something to his father, who stopped playing and spoke some urgent words.

For some time Jack listened, nodding, asking questions. At last he seemed to understand. Grigore gestured to include me. Jack looked reticent. "It seems," he said at last in a soft voice, "that the boy has the power of second sight." He could not withhold an embarrassed laugh.

I looked at Tomas. He was nodding, eager to communicate, his eyes earnest. "Is that right?" I said, for want of anything better.

"He wants to know." Jack hesitated again. "He wants to know if you see them, too."

The boy was watching me intently. He made a wide gesture toward the trees.

I hedged. "See what, exactly?"

Jack could only hide his disdain unconvincingly, so kept his head turned away from our companions as best he could. "It seems they believe that Purgatory is not some other place, as the Romans do, but that the spirits of unbaptized children walk among us, and can be seen particularly at this time of year. What is he calling it? A 'bend' or something. A 'hinge', I believe is the idea. A hinge in the year, when the ghouls appear."

His face was strained with withheld laughter. Underneath it, I saw the fear. He needed it to be ridiculous. I looked back at the others, calm and earnest in their desire to communicate. They felt his condescension, I'm sure of it, but didn't seem to mind very much. It is possible they thought him beneath their notice.

I ignored his need for me to laugh at them and nodded to Tomas. "Tell him it's interesting, and ask him if the dead children want something from us."

That question sobered Jack right up. After some back and forth he said, "He says the children will not bother us. They are waiting for the world to end, which will happen when the moon bleeds and the sun darkens." His voice was filled with open contempt now.

I traded smiles with the boy, nodded at him, and made an Indian hand-gesture from home which indicated the successful conclusion to an interaction. It's used to signal a deal done, a message received, an understanding shared, a peace brokered. He nodded with some enthusiasm and spoke softly with his father, then mimicked the sign back to me with a genuine smile.

Jack has his uses, I don't deny it, but only when he's tucked up safe inside his medical bag. Here's a true thing: put a scientific modernist, a peasant, a priest, and a small child into a haunted house. The modernist will be so scared that the other three will spend half the night soothing him. Then, in the morning, he'll deny that anything happened.

Our Slavic friends have turned back, and we are on our own. The farther we ride, the stranger the place becomes.

Chimera surround us here. It's not just the wolves, which shadow us in packs as we move, waiting for us to falter. Dark, bestial shapes, I swear, hunker in trees and dive in swooping flight overhead. There's a constant feeling that the darkness of the land itself is gathering, closing in, to envelop us. The land itself feels hungry.

In the old days, Jorgao talked some about his homeland. There were gods and spirits for every grove, even for each tree. Certainly every body of water was considered a borderland place, a mouth into another world. There was one god who wore his feet on backwards to foil trackers, and let out a high whistle so uncanny it drove men mad. I don't recall his Brazilian name, but it translated to "man of blisters."

I could have slept more comfortably never having heard of the Man of Blisters.

One time Jorgao came with me when I crossed the border into Texas. Not to visit. We were re-outfitting and I had the usual weary business among bankers and lawyers to attend. Since Mexicans were still squinted at, and few Texans would dignify a difference between any dark-skinned man from south of the Rio Grande, we slept under the sky in out of the way places, of which I knew many, and kept largely to ourselves.

After a tedious day at the bank, I rode back out to our camp where he was roasting squirrels for supper. I settled in to our customary silence, but I suppose I was ashamed of my countrymen, so by way of working up to an apology I asked him his opinion of Texas.

"Strange place," he said. "No demons here."

It surprised me to hear it, and I said so.

"No demons who walk free," he clarified. "Since the people here are asleep, the demons can ride them easy, and they don't even know they're being ridden."

The end-battle is upon us.

We now travel in so close an alignment to the Count's gypsies that when our trail veers toward the main road, we hear the creaking of their wagon, the nervous protests of their horses, the guttural exchanges shouted above the winds, now snow-laced, which is cause for some concern.

The thing must be done before winter takes firm hold, or we'll never make it out alive.

I can feel the thing, feel it near. I can smell it on the crisp air. With luck, Art and Harker will pull up to bolster our attack, but, one way or the other, tomorrow will be the day for blood.

This is the last entry I will make in this *libro malefico*.

If we are successful in tomorrow's adventure, I will burn the damned thing.

If we are not, well, then here you are, my unfortunate reader, taking its burden upon yourself. I suppose it is meant as a sort of apology for a life lived very badly indeed. If it strikes you that I'm making excuses, wringing my hands and blaming my dark affliction for all my misdeeds, then I'm telling it wrong, as that is not at all my intention.

Even we accursed make our choices. I know that. Cursed or not, it all lands on me, this whole, unholy life of mine.

Editor's Note

Here ends Morris' testament. The only parts I've omitted I find illegible. I still have the original, however, and will happily make it available to any scholar willing to try his hand at translating the smudges and scrawls.

PERTINENT
DOCUMENTS

Publisher's Note

The following were either included with the manuscript by Mr. Harker, or, as noted, added through research done here at the publishing house.

Fragment copied from a letter from Mrs. Wilhelmina Harker to her son

3 November 1904

My dearest darling – a short note to commemorate your twelfth birthday...

...As always, our thoughts on the day will be both of our son and his namesake, that brave man who gave his life to vanquish a terrible evil, these thirteen years past, on this very day. If only you might have known him, I'm certain you would love him as your father and I have done.

Quincey Morris will always be the template I hold in my mind for the Great Warrior. Whenever I read of Achilles or Hector, of Hannibal or Alexander the Great, it is the person of Quincey Morris who stands forth in my mind's eye, wearing the clothes of those great men. Indeed, I remember witnessing once as he fought the Count's minions, and they like locusts, it was a terrible sight, but he never wavered. When his rifle emptied, he threw it aside and pulled his revolver. When that was done, he used it as a club, then pulled his great knife and left a trail of death in its wake. Does this sound morbid? I suppose it does – forgive your mother! The thing I want to communicate is that I will swear, as I watched him, that he seemed to be doubled. It was as if his own shadow fought alongside him, slashing and clubbing, echoing his every move…

Sometimes, when I look suddenly at you from the corner of my eyes, my darling boy, I do think I see him in you…

Letter from Dr. John Seward to Jonathan Harker

30 APRIL 1897

My dear Harker:

You ask me to put forward an account of our final evening – Morris' and mine – leading to the fateful encounter with the beast himself. You do not offer your reasons for inquiring, all these many years later, but I suppose in your role as archives-keeper to the whole sordid business, you will want as complete a record as may be had.

Very well. Here it is, as well as memory may retain it.

As you will recall, Morris and I set out along the mountainous bank of the river, riding fast with extra horses and, later, when it became necessary, a sledge to carry our weapons and stores up the increasingly difficult Carpathian ridges. The snow had begun, of course, but we – Morris in particular – were no strangers to hard travel, and we went smoothly enough.

Our last night was passed in a rocky grotto, a sort of natural sanctuary set between boulders where we set our tents and struck up our fire and settled in for the night. The wolves presented a danger – you will remember as well as I the fearsome massing of their strange and wavering song – so we kept the fire burning hot along the edge of our encampment all night. In fact, at his insistence, we dismantled the sledge itself, using its wood for kindling. "After tonight," he said, in his stoical fashion, "we'll no longer require it, one way or the other."

He took the first watch, and, indeed, let me sleep longer than I ought. You ask if I'd seen him keeping a record, and the answer is yes. Night-times, he wrote. I rather teased him about it once, about setting aside his Winchester by night to wield instead the uncharacteristic quill. He gave me half a smile and claimed to be "tying up loose ends," which I took to mean he was writing letters, settling his affairs, et cetera, in case the worst should happen, which, God rest him, turned out to be prophecy. I don't know what came of the letters. I suppose they must have been duly posted upon our return through Budapest. Do you know, Harker?

The three of us – Morris and Godalming and I – had travelled in company on more than one prior occasion, and I feel confident in saying that there was little else in his manner which stood apart from his usual, pragmatic method. One thing only: when I woke, not long before dawn, to find that he had let me oversleep my hour, he was standing over his bearskin. You remember the one: a trophy he had taken early in life, "a grizz from the Rockies" he called it, and carried this skin with him everywhere, used it for bedding or warmth or decoration on every expedition I knew him to take, even into the heat of the jungle or desert. He told me that one aboriginal tribe near his home in Texas bestowed upon him the name of "Mupitz-Vuh", meaning I suppose something akin to "great hunter of bear", since the skin was so entirely his identifying mark. *

*{*EDITOR'S NOTE: According to Professor Algernon B. Swindells of Kings College, Oxford, "muupits" is a*

Comanche term for "monster". In personal correspondence,
he speculates that the suffix "-vuh" is an intensifier, in
effect exaggerating the monstrosity of the described.}

In the event, it was spread across the ground and he
stood over it holding the little keg in which we kept
our salt, scattering the salt-crystals across it. It struck
me as odd, but he was the more seasoned traveler of
us two, so I assumed it was to some practical purpose.
I did inquire, to which he repeated: "Loose ends, Doc,
loose ends." Then, curiously, he rolled the beloved
old bearskin up and shoved it onto the fire. It was
an unthinkable gesture, particularly on so wretchedly
cold a night. I began to protest, but was quieted by
an idea that perhaps he'd had some premonition of
approaching death, and was acting accordingly. They
do say such things happen. Scientist though I am, I
will allow that so skilled a hunter as Quincey Morris
might have some notion when he has met the prey
which will ultimately best him.

You know the rest. We rode from the south, you and
Godalming circled round from the north, we converged
upon the Count's Szgany with their baleful cargo, and
the rest, as Morris might have said, is "cut and dried."

I trust you and your own little Quincey – not so
little anymore, eh? – are keeping well. I still visit
Lucy's grave regularly, did you know? and, while there,
I always cast a thought to your own lovely Mina, to
the very masculinity of her courage and fortitude. We
should not have survived it without her, should we?
Please pass onto her my fondest regards.

Your affectionate comrade-at-arms,
John L. Seward, MD

Letter from Professor Abraham Van Helsing to Quincey Harker

4 SEPTEMBER 1912

My Dear Young Master Harker:

You astonish me with your revelations. I ought perhaps to be ashamed that I overlooked such hidden monstrousness in one of our own intimate party. In my defense I say, whether to the good or no, that Morris was an American, and the American is deceptive in the simplicity of his seeming. He spoke little, Morris, and when he was in a mood to hold forth, he did so in jargon designed to amuse his continental listeners. Perhaps this was means to mask his shadow. Also and however, we must not be quick to forget that nobility of bearing and courage of spirit which were most assuredly his own, as much as, or more than, this soi-disant monstrousness of which he speaks.

He fought, as they say, his own demons. What man can say he has not? It is when this fight is abnegated, then and only then is the man at fault, and Morris was a fighter, brave and true, to the end.

This much being spoken, I am given some pause as I recollect. Please recall the final battle against the vampire, the details of which I am certain that you, as heir to your parents' legacy, have long been privy. In the last moments of sunlight, while the creature lay still powerless within his coffin, the young men of our party fought courageously against his mercenaries, first with the Winchester, then at close quarters with knife and revolver. During this skirmish, Morris took his mortal side-wound. Just at the crucial moment when our safeguard, the sun, was slipping away and the beast was about to revive into life, Morris and your father prised open the box and, in one instant (I know this because your mother and I watched these proceedings most fretfully through field-glasses), your father sawed the creature's head from its neck while Morris plunged his great rhino-head knife through its black heart, and we watched in amazement as an ancient evil crumbled into a few fistfuls of dust.

We have long given mutual credit to both men, but now I think me, if one cared to split the hair, the achievement belonged to your father alone. The nosferatu is an odd animal, his tenacious hold on life such that he can be ended only in very specific ways. The decapitation, yes, or by fire, or sunlight. The bullet, drowning, dearth of air, a fall from great height, these terrible fatalities affect him not. Even starvation, in my experience, will not end him, but change his undead nature into something more vegetable: an undernourished vampire will shrivel and become still, not unlike one of those snapping plants in the darks of the jungle which lure their nourishment into the mouth since they cannot pursue it elsewise.

My point, dear boy, is this: a wooden stake through the vampire's heart, or the place the heart once has beaten, is a sure and well-tried means of its demise. Metal, however, has no such proven transformative effect, unless it is first sanctified in holy water. In short, your father killed Dracula by removing the ancient head from the ancient neck. Had only Morris reached the beast at that moment, the knife might have slowed him, but the evil would still be among us, undead, and feeding. Worse, your mother, I fear to say, would not have survived that terrible night.

Well, but I am now nearly as ancient as the beast was then, and these ruminations of mine may be faulty and unfair. Why desecrate the name of a man long dead? I ask this question not to dissuade you from your stated purpose of bringing these newfound papers to light, but merely as the philosophical musings of a very old man.

All good luck to you from your ancient friend,
VH

Editor's Postscript

Little can be added to so extraordinary an account. For my own part, I was born on the anniversary of Quincey Morris's death at the hands of Dracula's gypsies, and my sweet mother never let a birthday pass without reminding me that, in her opinion, some part of that great hunter's spirit had passed into me.

This has afforded me, in light of this document, some occasion for dark reflection. Morris never relates – indeed, never seems to have known – exactly what "dark thing from another century" was "alive within his own flesh." If he was right in his conjecture, if his worst deeds were accomplished not solely of his own accord but with the assistance of some foul, possessing force, what happens to such a parasite at the death of its host? Where does it go?

These thoughts trouble me.

I submit to the perusal of the world, without further remark, this transcript of darkness.

Quincey Harker, May 1914

Publisher's Addendum

These documents were received all in a bundle at this publishing house in the summer of 1914, just as the civilized world was headed into chaos. Mr. Quincey Harker, being a young gentleman of sound body, joined up to fight for his country and was listed missing in action at Mametz Wood during first Somme, presumed dead.

Letter to publisher from The Office Ministry of War

14 May 1920

Dear Sir:

In respect to your enquiry of December last year, we regret to inform you that 2nd Lt. Quincey Harker, late of the Royal Welch Fusiliers, was declared missing and is presumed dead during the early days of the Somme Offensive in July 1916.

Until his disappearance, the deceased served faithfully and was renowned as fierce and unwavering in attack. He seems to have left no family, and because you are the only friend of his to step forward, I enclose a copy of the original telegram declaring him missing.

His remains have never been recovered, nor his person found.

Following the Armistice, an official commission was formed to investigate the whereabouts of soldiers misplaced during that terrible engagement. No leads were found as pertain to your friend.

In his file, however, I find a memorandum which might be of interest. It is from Maj.-Gen. Ivor Philipps, who had, that very week in July, been replaced as Harker's C.O., so had no information to share concerning the disappearance, but enjoyed some acquaintance with the man himself. The pertinent passage runs as follows:

ιs to your insinuation, Harker was not the man ιun. He was infamous amongst his comrades for rocious feats of courage, and for his berserker-ιke fury in battle when loosed against the Hun. I recall on one occasion having had to reprimand him when, during an early nocturnal engagement – this is prior to the Somme, of course – he sprang from his entrenchment before the order was given. I still see him quite vividly, a figure almost blurred in constant motion, silhouetted against the harsh fireworks of the bombardment, the tail of his ever-present raccoon-cap adding a comic bounce, streaking like a demon into the hell of No-Man's-Land whilst uttering that ghostly howling which was his particular signature, or emblem.

"…He more than once appeared to me in those times to be standing doubled, as if the soldier were twinned by a doppelganger. Optical illusions are not uncommon against the strange lighting and high pique of the battlefield, and this was no doubt one, consisting of some kind of shadow effect which appeared fur-capped and howling and ferocious as its original…"

I know that Harker's name was put forth on more than one occasion for the DSO. I am unable to glean the reasons why the requests never bore fruit.

It is my sincerest hope that these intelligences will assist you in coming to terms with the loss of your friend. If you find him, do by all means let us know, so that we may update our records.

I am, sir, your servant,

Lt. Reginald Howe
Office of Records, Ministry of War

THE THREE BOOKS
by
Paul StJohn Mackintosh

"I've been told that this is the most elegant thing I've ever written. I can't think how such a dark brew of motifs came together to create that effect. But there's unassuaged longing and nostalgia in here, interwoven with the horror, as well as an unflagging drive towards the final consummation. I still feel more for the story's characters, whether love or loathing, than for any others I've created to date. Tragedy, urban legend, Gothic romance, warped fairy tale of New York: it's all there. And of course, most important of all is the seductive allure of writing and of books – and what that can lead some people to do.

You may not like my answer to the mystery of the third book. But I hope you stay to find out."

Paul StJohn Mackintosh

"Paul StJohn Mackintosh is one of those writers who just seems to quietly get on with the business of producing great fiction... it's an excellent showcase for his obvious talents. His writing, his imagination, his ability to lay out a well-paced and intricate story in only 100 pages is a great testament to his skills."

—This is Horror

Also from BLACK SHUCK *Signature*

BLACK STAR, BLACK SUN
by
Rich Hawkins

"Black Star, Black Sun *is my tribute to Lovecraft, Ramsey Campbell, and the haunted fields of Somerset, where I seemed to spend much of my childhood. It's a story about going home and finding horror there when something beyond human understanding begins to invade our reality. It encompasses broken dreams, old memories, lost loved ones and a fundamentally hostile universe. It's the last song of a dying world before it falls to the Black Star."*

Rich Hawkins

"Black Star, Black Sun *possesses a horror energy of sufficient intensity to make readers sit up straight. A descriptive force that shifts from the raw to the nuanced. A ferocious work of macabre imagination and one for readers of Conrad Williams and Gary McMahon."*
—Adam Nevill, author of *The Ritual*

"Reading Hawkins' novella is like sitting in front of a guttering open fire. Its glimmerings captivate, hissing with irrepressible life, and then, just when you're most seduced by its warmth, it spits stinging embers your way. This is incendiary fiction. Read at arms' length."
—Gary Fry, author of *Conjure House*

blackshuckbooks.co.uk/signature

DEAD LEAVES

by

Andrew David Barker

"*This book is my love letter to the horror genre. It is about what it means to be a horror fan; about how the genre can nurture an adolescent mind; how it can be a positive force in life.*

This book is set during a time when horror films were vilified in the press and in parliament like never before. It is about how being a fan of so-called 'video nasties' made you, in the eyes of the nation, a freak, a weirdo, or worse, someone who could actually be a danger to society.

This book is partly autobiographical, set in a time when Britain seemed to be a war with itself. It is a working class story about hope. All writers, filmmakers, musicians, painters – artists of any kind –were first inspired to create their own work by the guiding light of another's. The first spark that sets them on their way.

This book is about that spark."

Andrew David Barker

———•———

"*Whilst Thatcher colluded with the tabloids to distract the public... an urban quest for the ultimate video nasty was unfolding, before the forces of media madness and power drunk politicians destroyed the Holy Grail of gore!*"

—Graham Humphreys, painter of *The Evil Dead* poster

THE FINITE
by
Kit Power

"The Finite *started as a dream; an image, really, on the edge of waking. My daughter and I, joining a stream of people walking past our house. We were marching together, and I saw that many of those behind us were sick, and struggling, and then I looked to the horizon and saw the mushroom cloud. I remember a wave of perfect horror and despair washing over me; the sure and certain knowledge that our march was doomed, as were we.*

The image didn't make it into the story, but the feeling did. King instructs us to write about what scares us. In The Finite, *I wrote about the worst thing I can imagine; my own childhood nightmare, resurrected and visited on my kid.*"

Kit Power

———•———

"The Finite *is* Where the Wind Blows *or* Threads *for the 21st century, played out on a tight scale by a father and his young daughter, which only serves to make it all the more heartbreaking.*"
—Priya Sharma, author of *Ormeshadow*

blackshuckbooks.co.uk/signature

RICOCHET
by
Tim Dry

"With Ricochet *I wanted to break away from the traditional linear form of storytelling in a novella and instead create a series of seemingly unrelated vignettes. Like the inconsistent chaos of vivid dreams I chose to create stand-alone episodes that vary from being fearful to blackly humorous to the downright bizarre. It's a book that you can dip into at any point but there is an underlying cadence that will carry you along, albeit in a strangely seductive new way.*

Prepare to encounter a diverse collection of characters. Amongst them are gangsters, dead rock stars, psychics, comic strip heroes and villains, asylum inmates, UFOs, occult nazis, parisian ghosts, decaying and depraved royalty and topping the bill a special guest appearance by the Devil himself."

Tim Dry

———•———

Reads like the exquisite lovechild of William Burroughs and Philip K. Dick's fiction, with some Ballard thrown in for good measure. Wonderfully imaginative, darkly satirical - this is a must read!
—Paul Kane, author of *Sleeper(s)* and *Ghosts*

blackshuckbooks.co.uk/signature

ROTH-STEYR
by
Simon Bestwick

"You never know which ideas will stick in your mind, let alone where they'll go. Roth-Steyr began with an interest in the odd designs and names of early automatic pistols, and the decision to use one of them as a story title. What started out as an oddball short piece became a much longer and darker tale about how easily a familiar world can fall apart, how old convictions vanish or change, and why no one should want to live forever.

It's also about my obsession with history, in particular the chaotic upheavals that plagued the first half of the twentieth century and that are waking up again. Another 'long dark night of the European soul' feels very close today.

So here's the story of Valerie Varden. And her Roth-Steyr."

Simon Bestwick

"A slice of pitch-black cosmic pulp, elegant and inventive in all the most emotionally engaging ways."

—Gemma Files, author of *In That Endlessness, Our End*

A DIFFERENT KIND OF LIGHT
by
Simon Bestwick

"When I first read about the Le Mans Disaster, over twenty years ago, I knew there was a story to tell about the newsreel footage of the aftermath – footage so appalling it was never released. A story about how many of us want to see things we aren't supposed to, even when we insist we don't.

What I didn't know was who would tell that story. Last year I finally realised: two lovers who weren't lovers, in a world that was falling apart. So at long last I wrote their story and followed them into a shadow land of old films, grief, obsession and things worse than death.

You only need open this book, and the film will start to play."

Simon Bestwick

———•———

"*Compulsively readable, original and chilling. Simon Bestwick's witty, engaging tone effortlessly and brilliantly amplifies its edge-of-your-seat atmosphere of creeping dread. I'll be sleeping with the lights on.*"

—Sarah Lotz, author of *The Three*, *Day Four*, *The White Road* & *Missing Person*

THE INCARNATIONS OF MARIELA PEÑA

by

Steven J Dines

"The Incarnations of Mariela Peña *is unlike anything I have ever written. It started life (pardon the pun) as a zombie tale and very quickly became something else: a story about love and the fictions we tell ourselves.*

During its writing, I felt the ghost of Charles Bukowski looking over my shoulder. I made the conscious decision to not censor either the characters or myself but to write freely and with brutal, sometimes uncomfortable, honesty. I was betrayed by someone I cared deeply for, and like Poet, I had to tell the story, or at least this incarnation of it. A story about how the past refuses to die."

Steven J Dines

———•———

"*Call it literary horror, call it psychological horror, call it a journey into the darkness of the soul. It's all here. As intense and compelling a piece of work as I've read in many a year.*"

—Paul Finch, author of *Kiss of Death* and *Stolen*,
and editor of the *Terror Tales* series.

blackshuckbooks.co.uk/signature

Also from BLACK SHUCK *Signature*

THE DERELICT
by
Neil Williams

"The Derelict *is really a story of two derelicts – the events on the first and their part in the creation of the second.*

With this story I've pretty much nailed my colours to the mast, so to speak. As the tale is intended as a tribute to stories by the likes of William Hope Hodgson or H P Lovecraft (with a passing nod to Coleridge's Ancient Mariner), where some terrible event is related in an unearthed journal or (as is the case here) by a narrator driven to near madness.

The primary influence on the story was the voyage of the Demeter, from Bram Stoker's Dracula, *one of the more compelling episodes of that novel. Here the crew are irrevocably doomed from the moment they set sail. There is never any hope of escape or salvation once the nature of their cargo becomes apparent. This was to be my jumping off point with* The Derelict.

Though I have charted a very different course from the one taken by Stoker, I have tried to remain resolutely true to the spirit of that genre of fiction and the time in which it was set."

Neil Williams

———•———

"*Fans of supernatural terror at sea will love* The Derelict. *I certainly did.*"
—Stephen Laws, author of *Ferocity* and *Chasm*

blackshuckbooks.co.uk/signature